Deborah Muller Coloring Bo
ChubbyMermaidArt.com

Thank you for choosing this coloring book. I hope you enjoy this book and have as much fun coloring in it as I did creating it for you. I appreciate your support.

Celebrate the Seasons

Girls to color through t the year

It truly brings me joy to see your wonderful masterpieces, please tag me #Deborahmullerart. Join me on Facebook at Deborah Muller's Coloring Group and show off your work.

Copyright material, all rights reserved. No parts of this book may be reproduced or sold without written permission.

ChubbyMermaidArt.com
Deborah Muller

This book belongs to me:

Name: _____

Nickname: _____

Birthplace: _____

Hometown: _____

Favorite Color: _____

Favorite Food: _____

Favorite Movie: _____

Favorite Drink: _____

Pets Names: _____

Favorite Song: _____

ChubbyMermaidArt.com
Deborah Muller

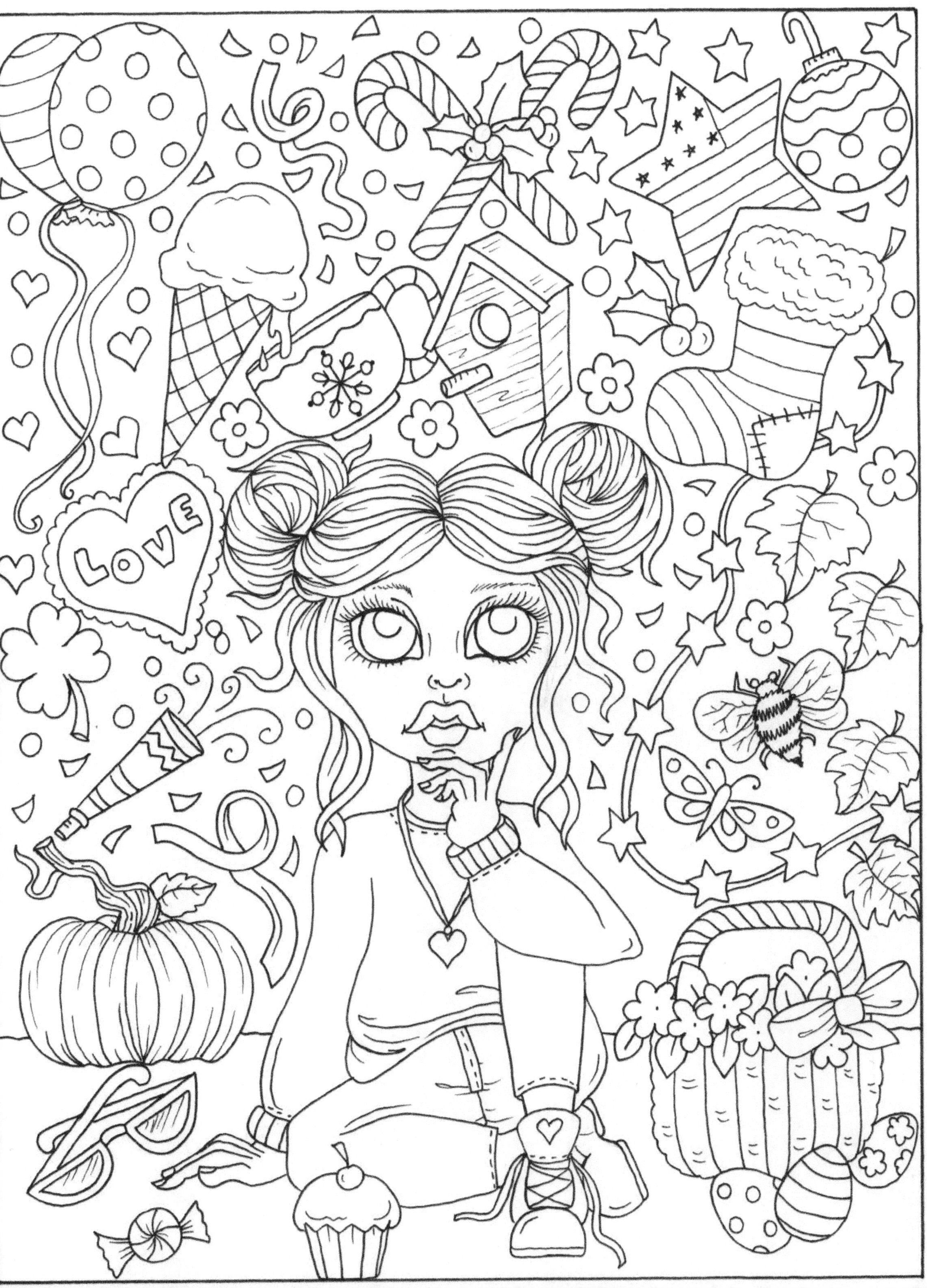
LOVE

JANUARY

NOTES

My Color Palette

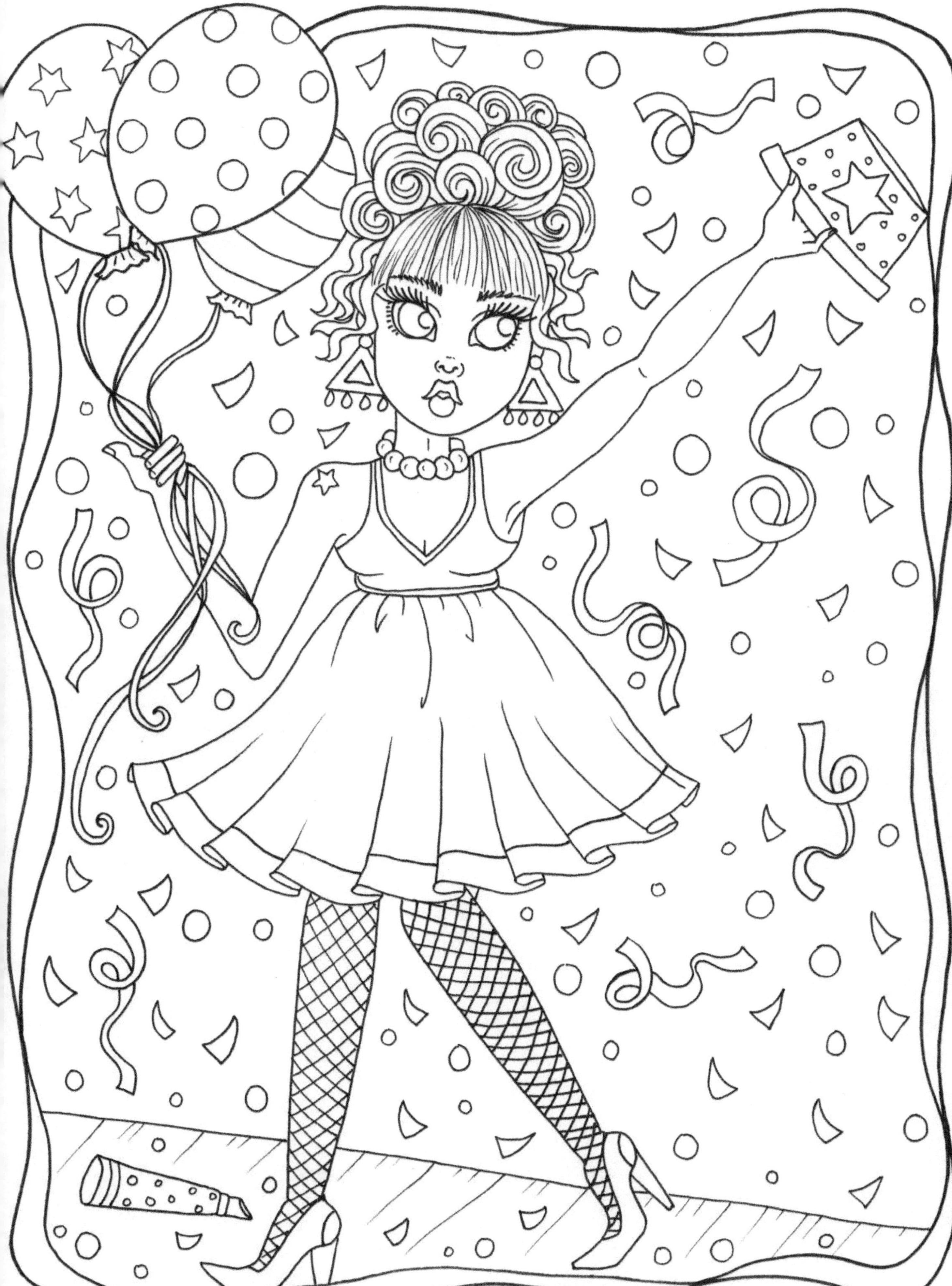

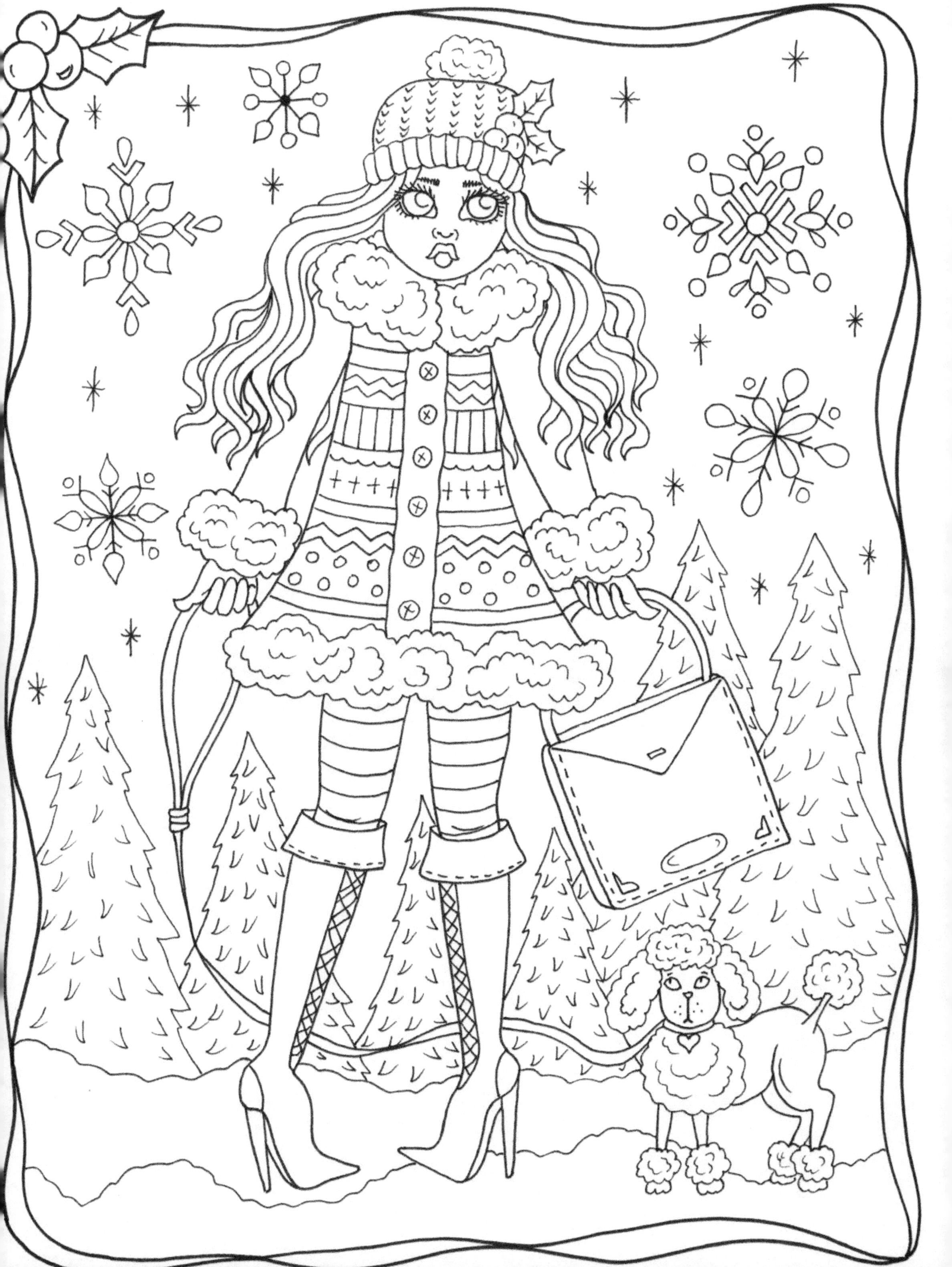

FEBRUARY

NOTES

My Color Palette

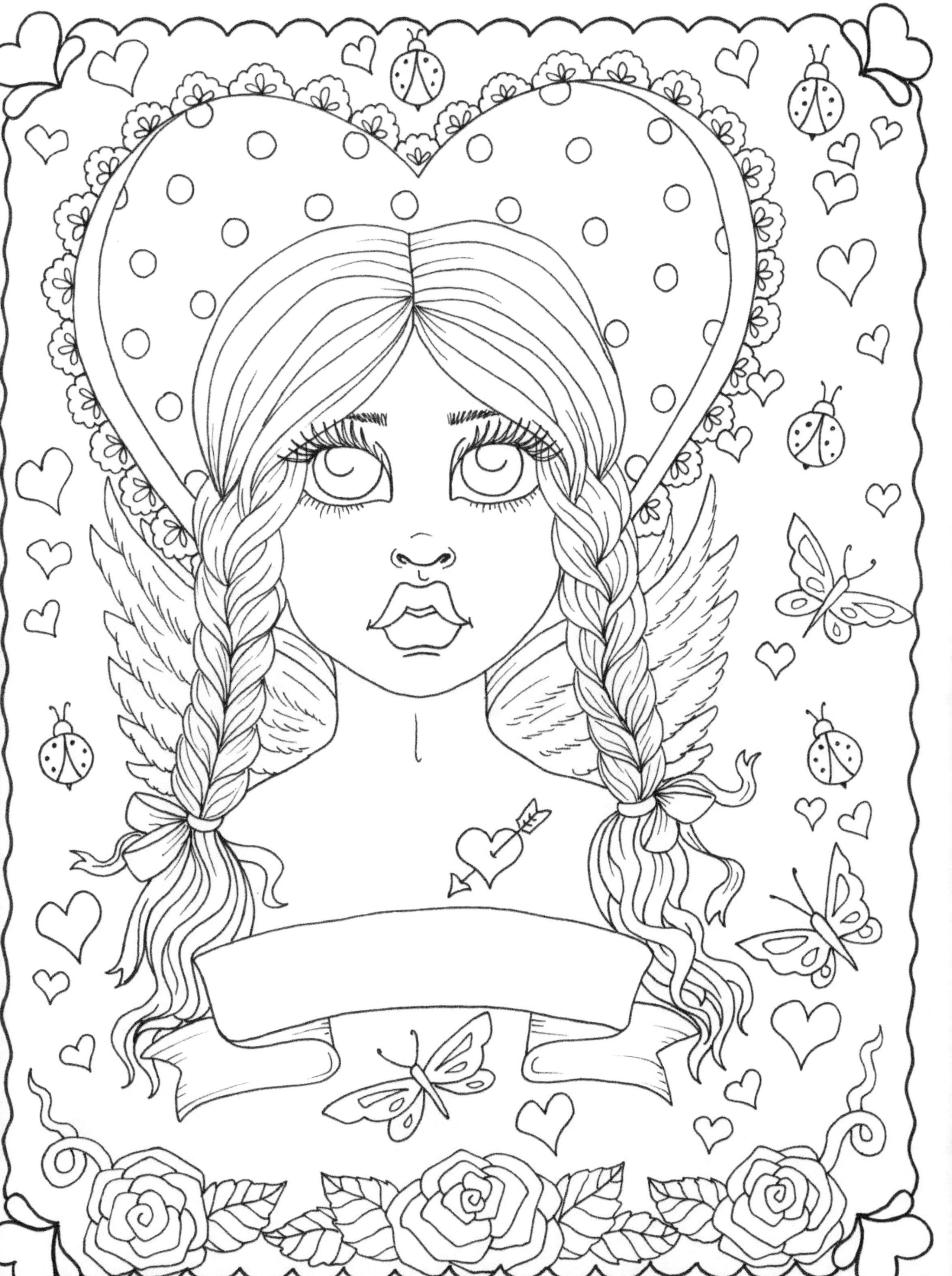

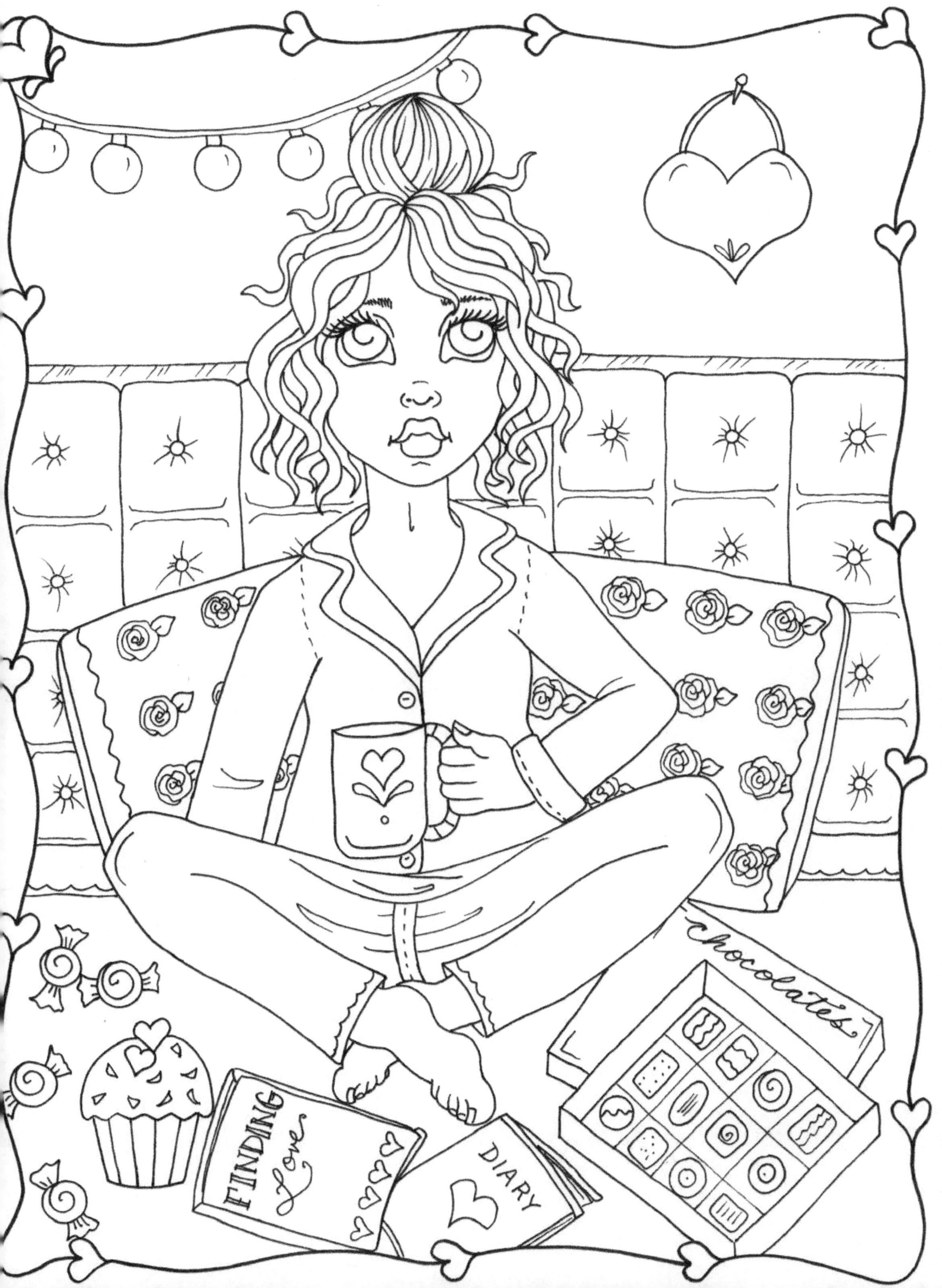
Chocolates
FINDING
Love
DIARY

MARCH

NOTES

My Color Palette

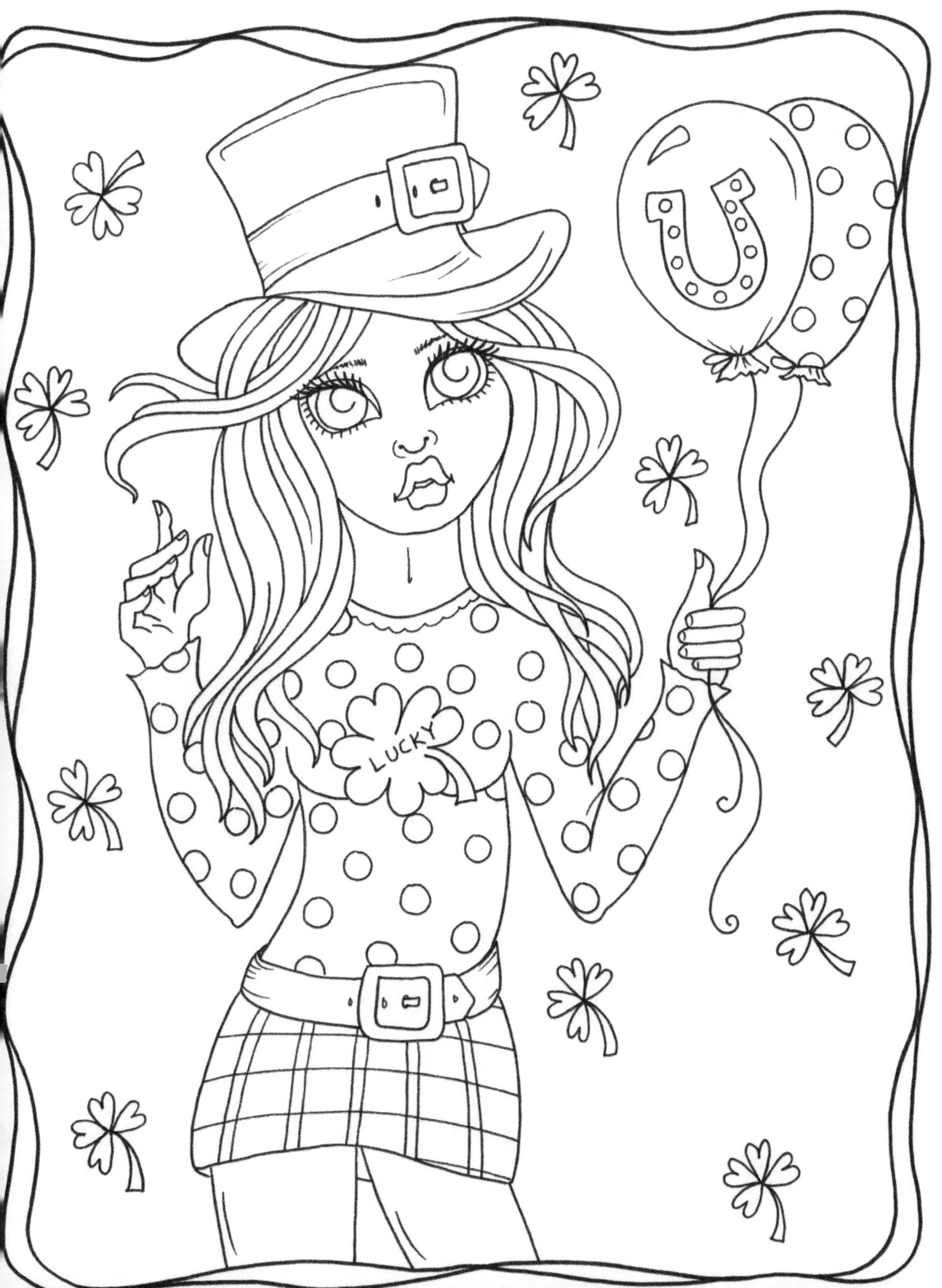
LUCKY

HOME sweet HOME

APRIL

NOTES

My Color Palette

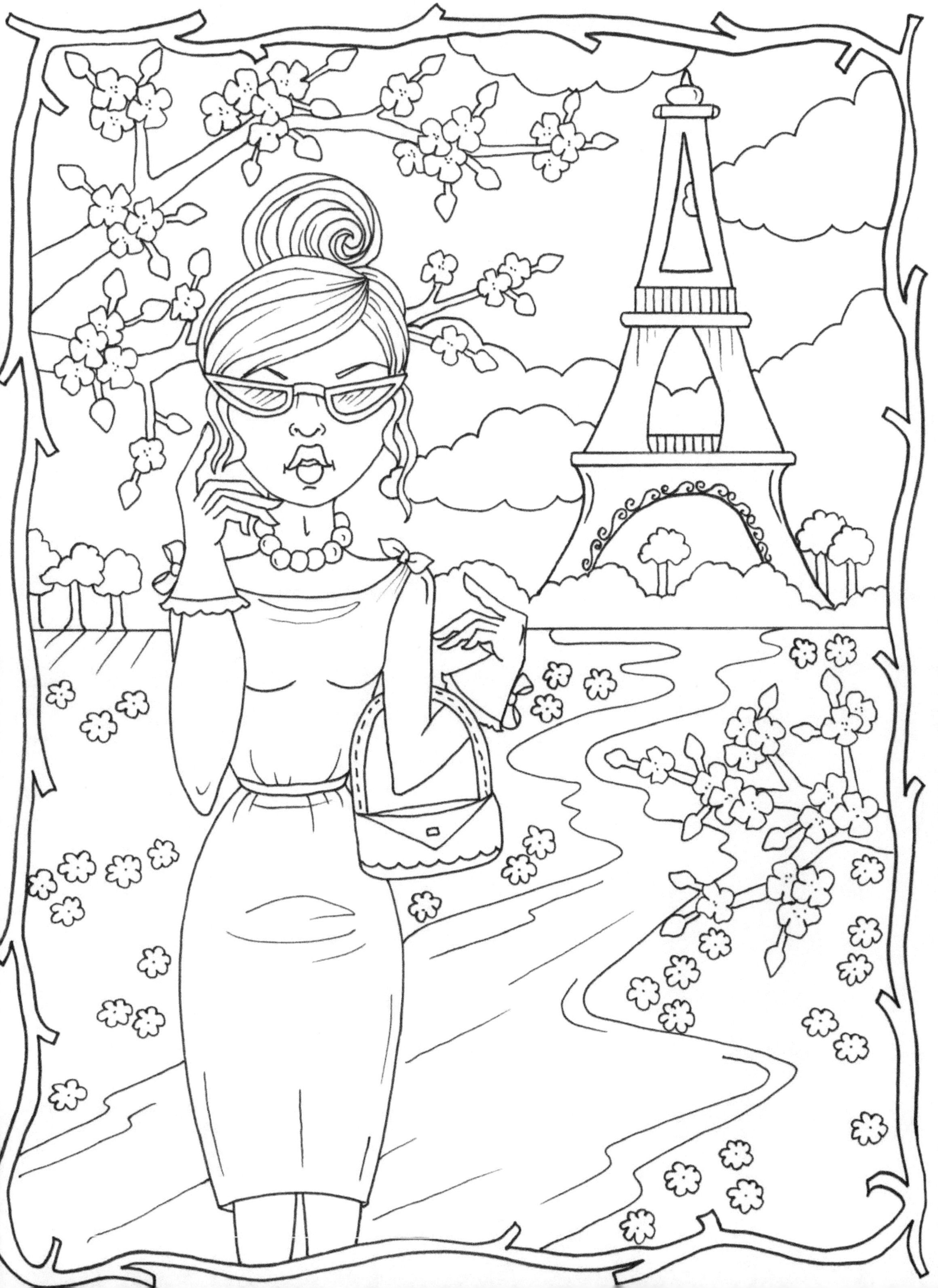

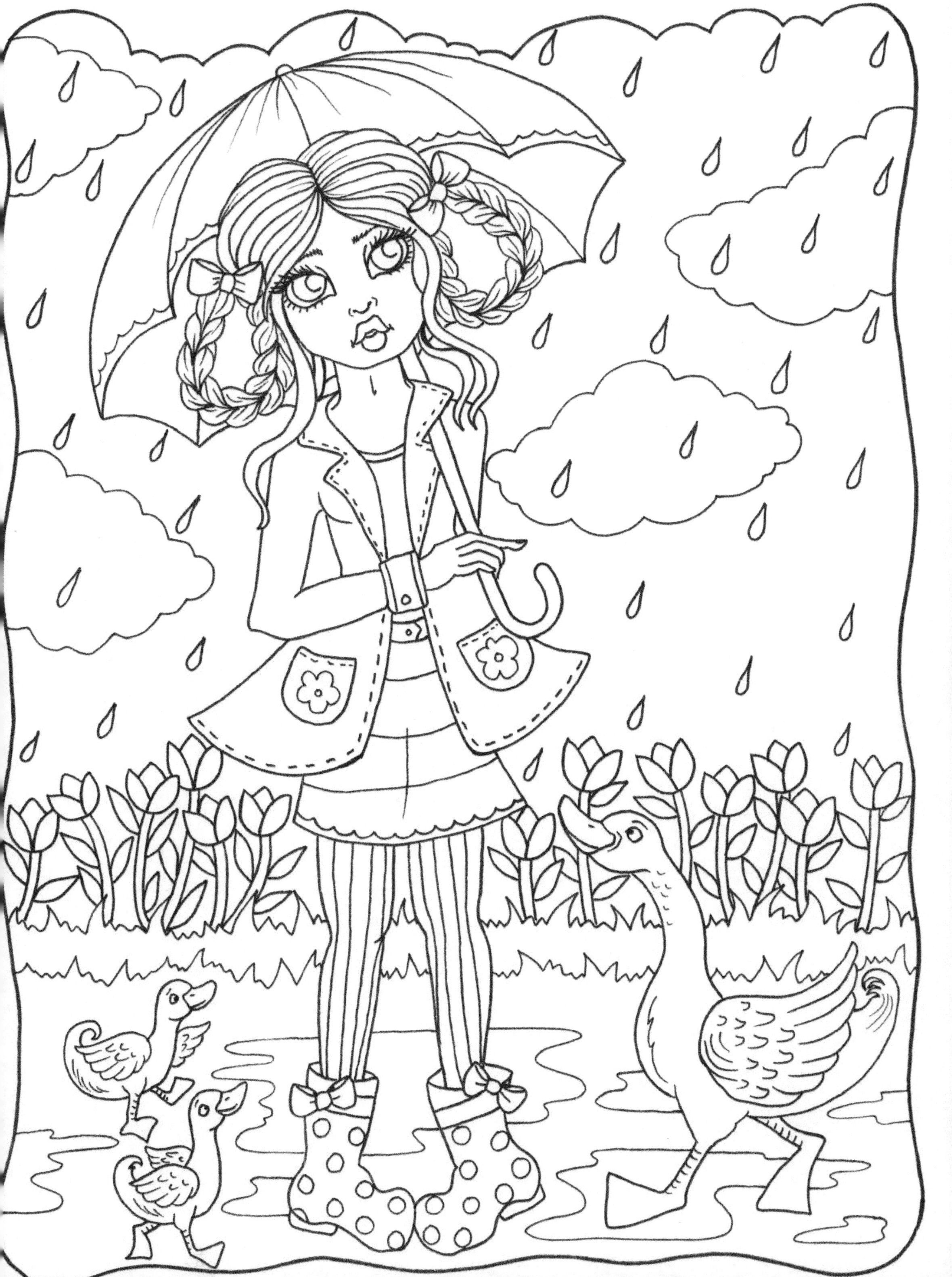

May

Notes

My Color Palette

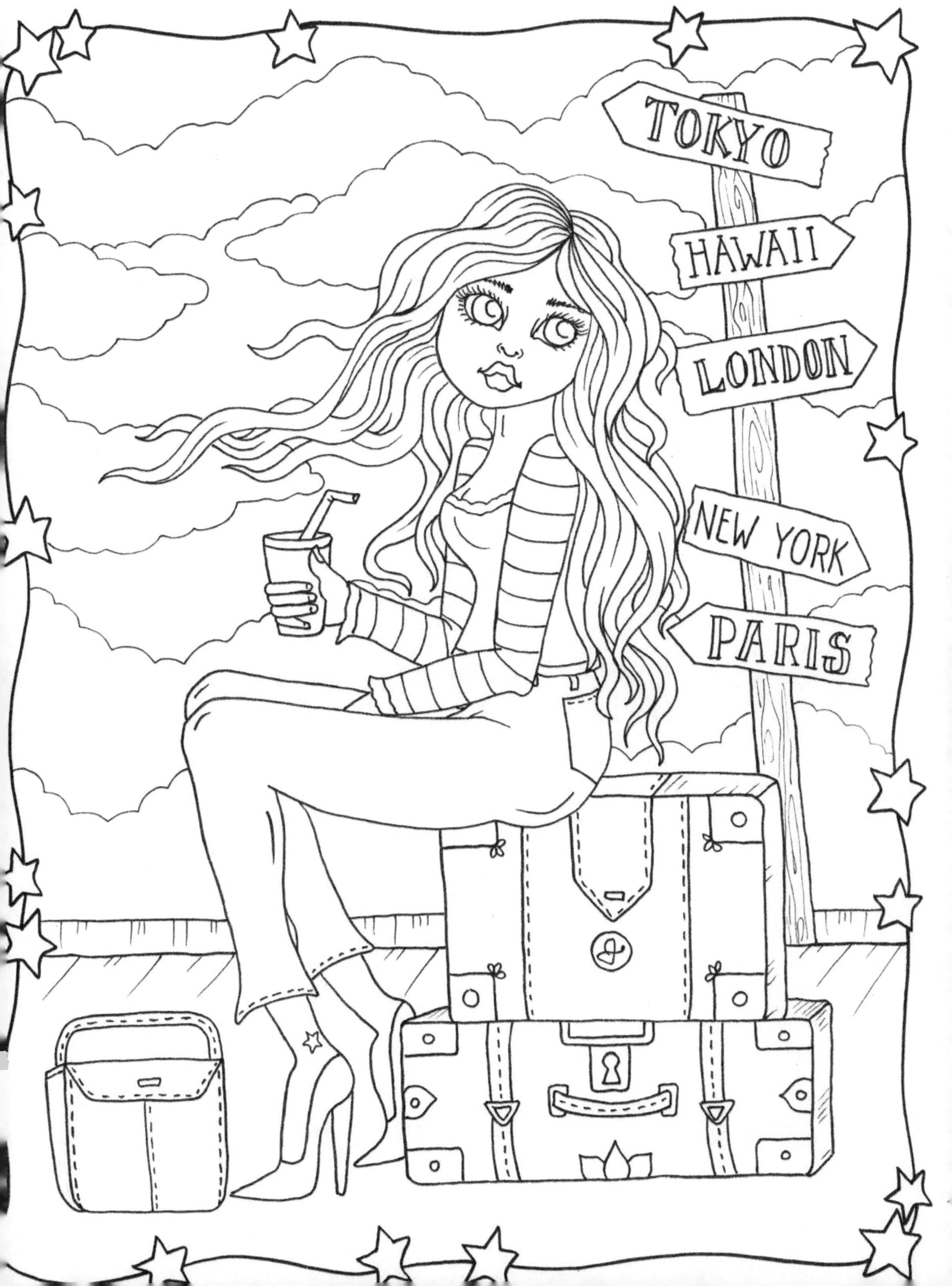
TOKYO
HAWAII
LONDON
NEW YORK
PARIS

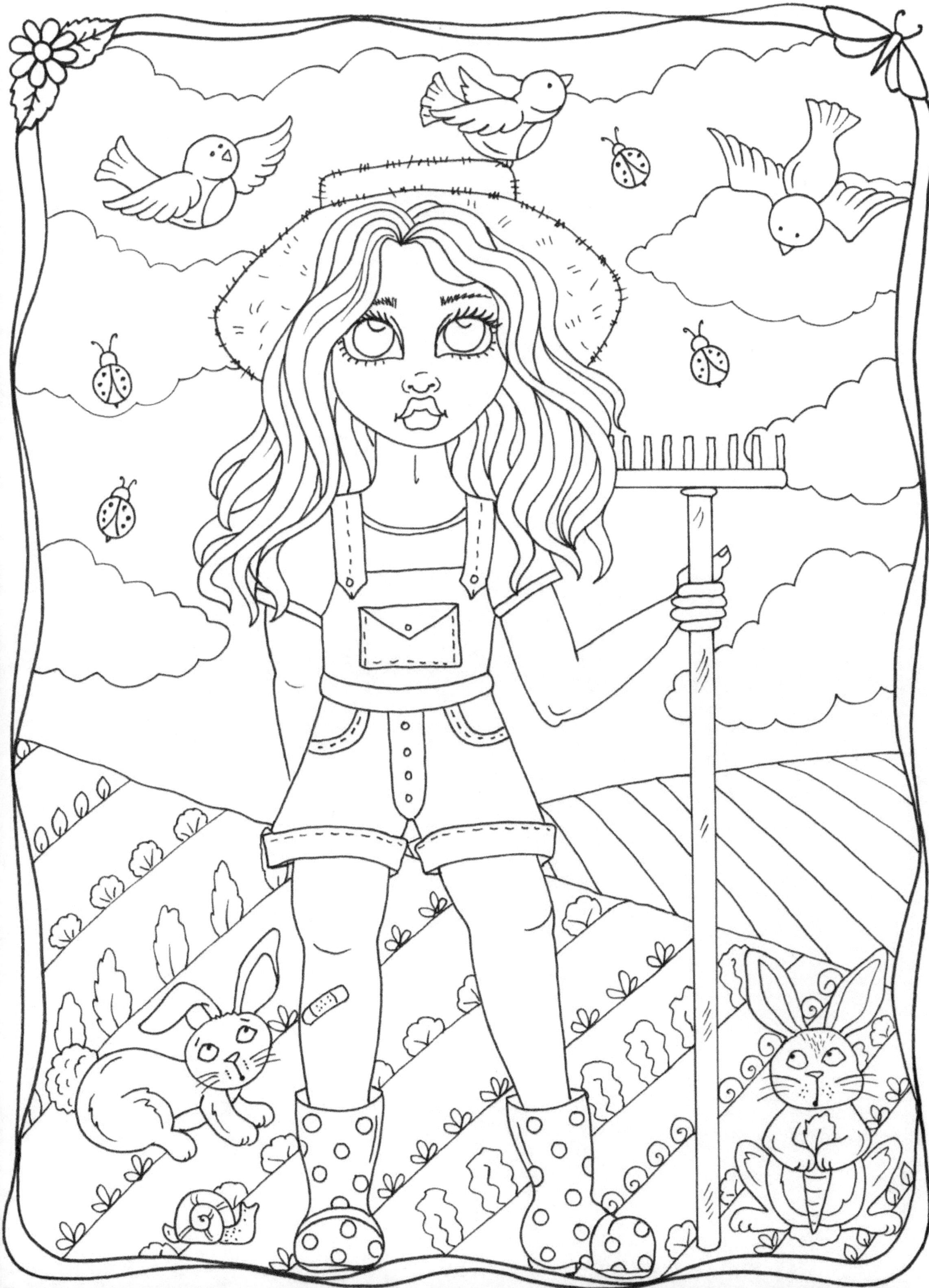

JUNE

NOTES

My Color Palette

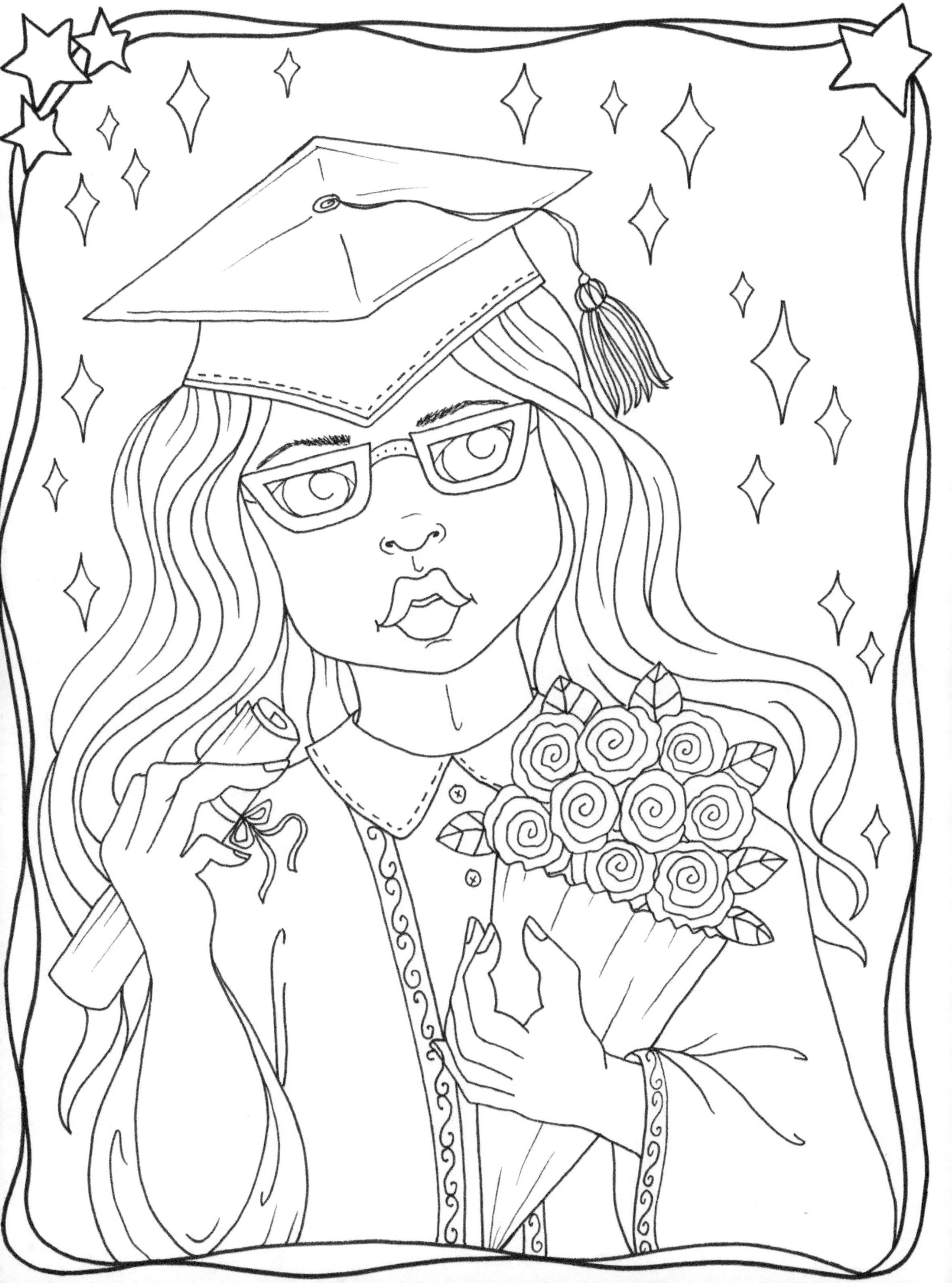

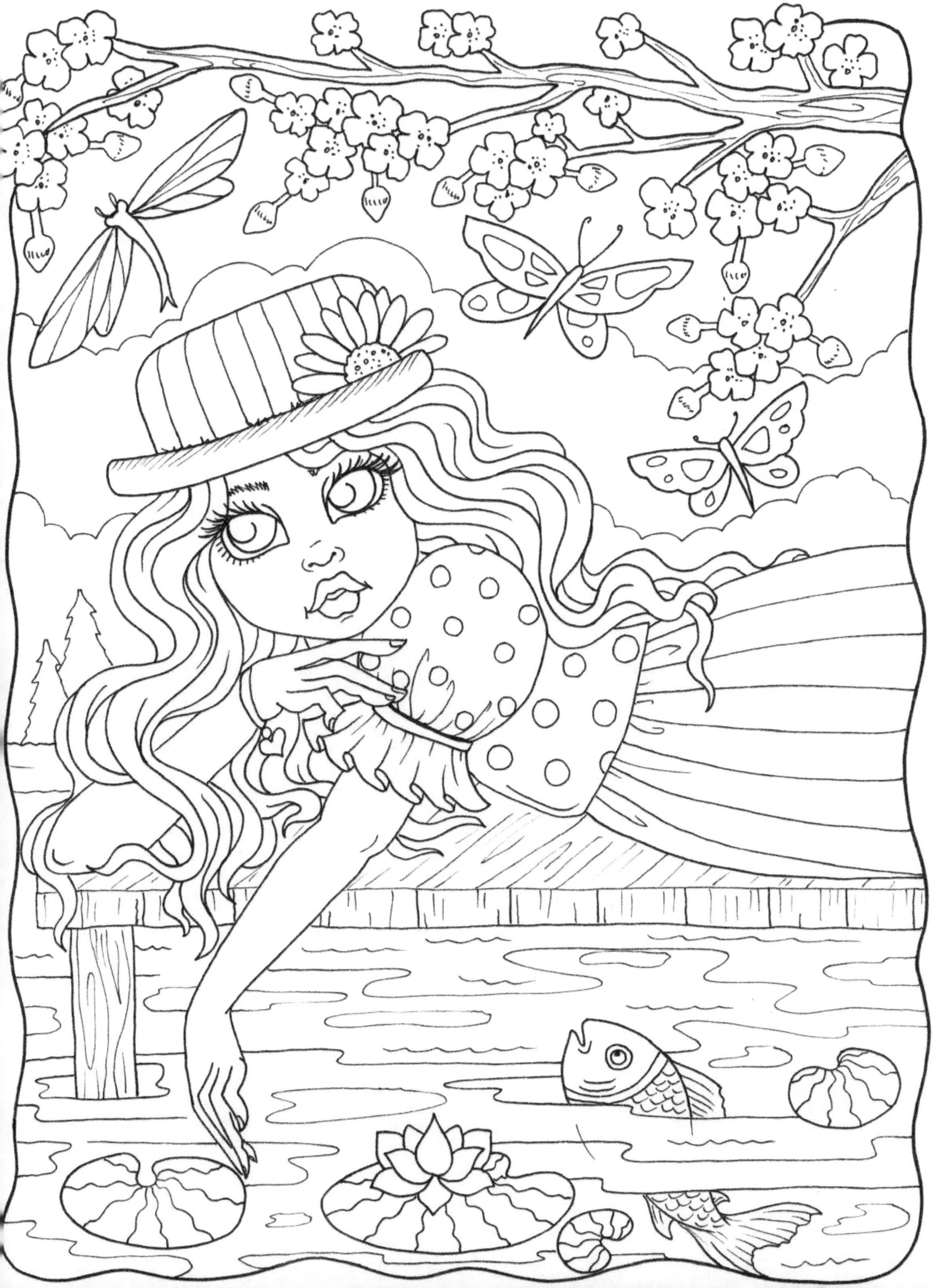

JULY

NOTES

My Color Palette

FREEDOM

USA

WORMS

AUGUST

NOTES

My Color Palette

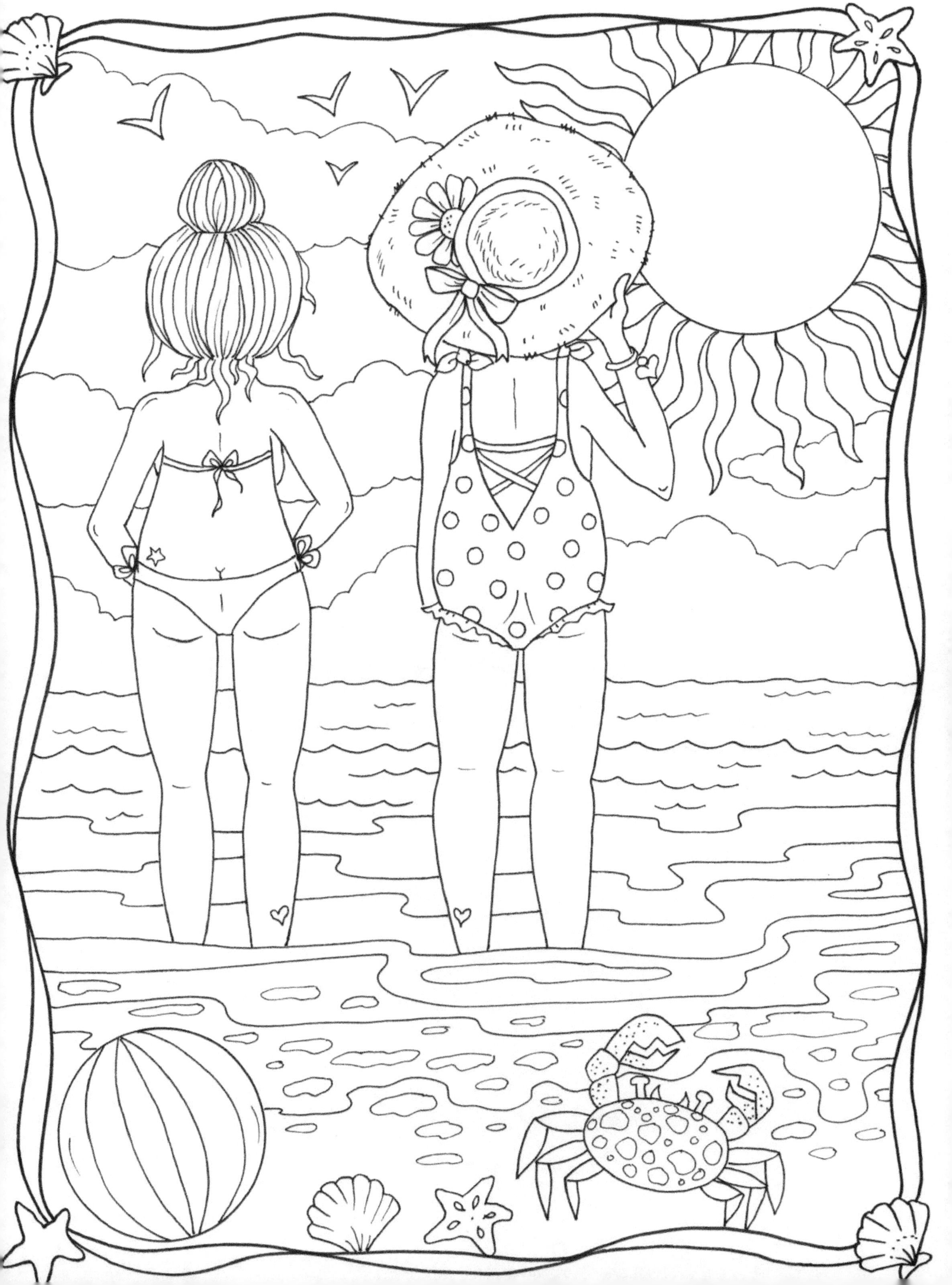

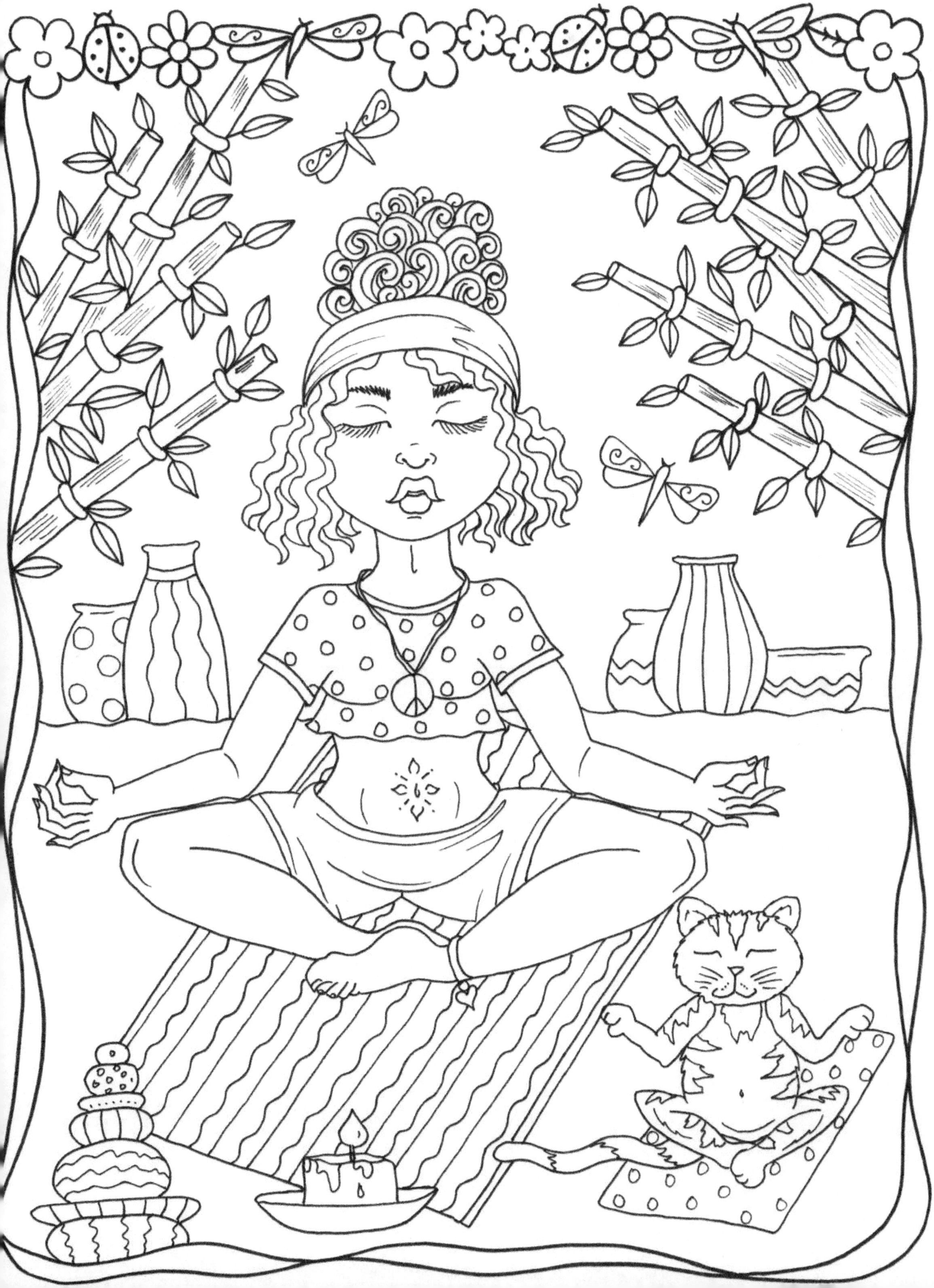

SEPTEMBER

NOTES

My Color Palette

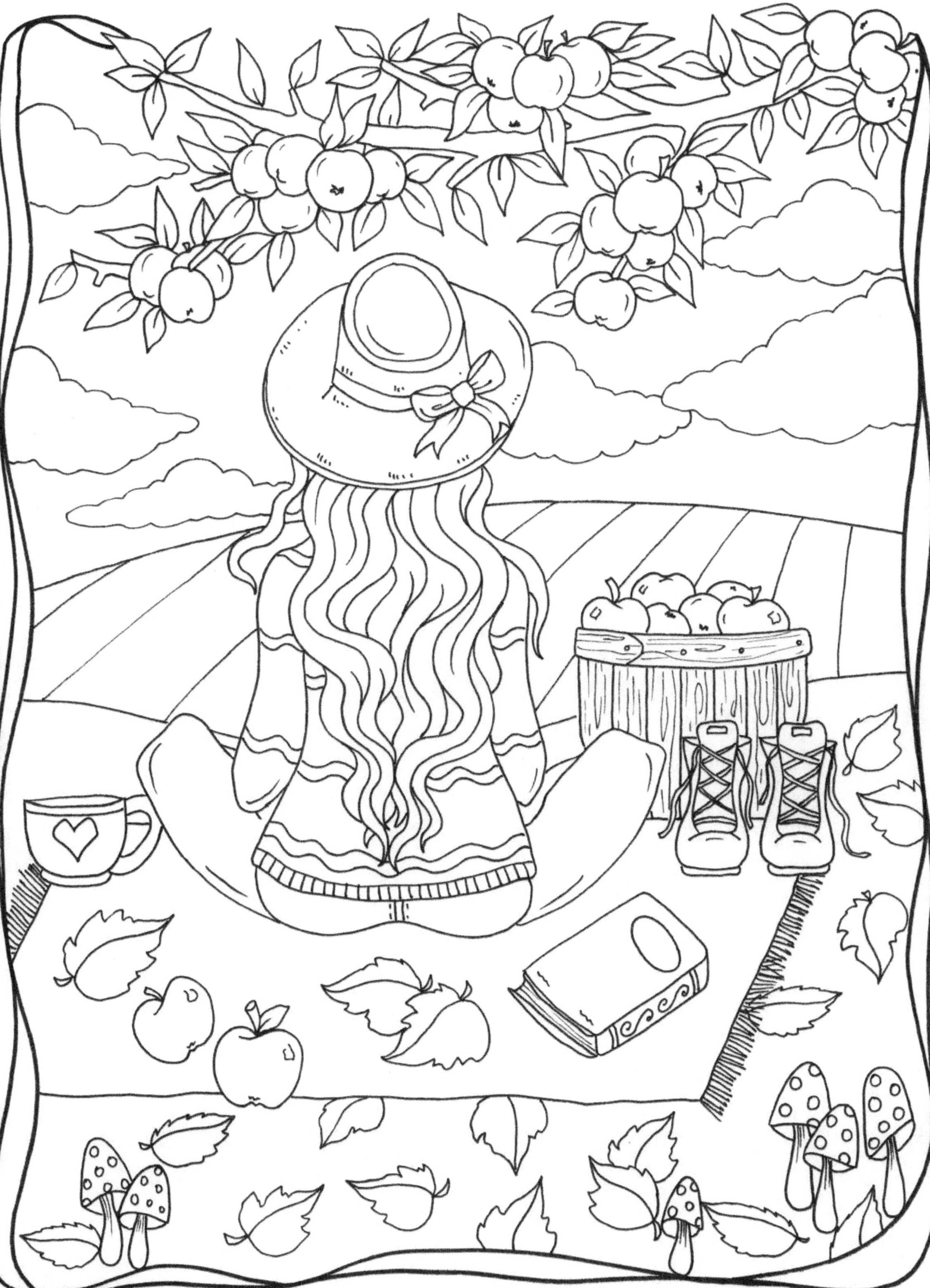

HOME

OCTOBER

NOTES

My Color Palette

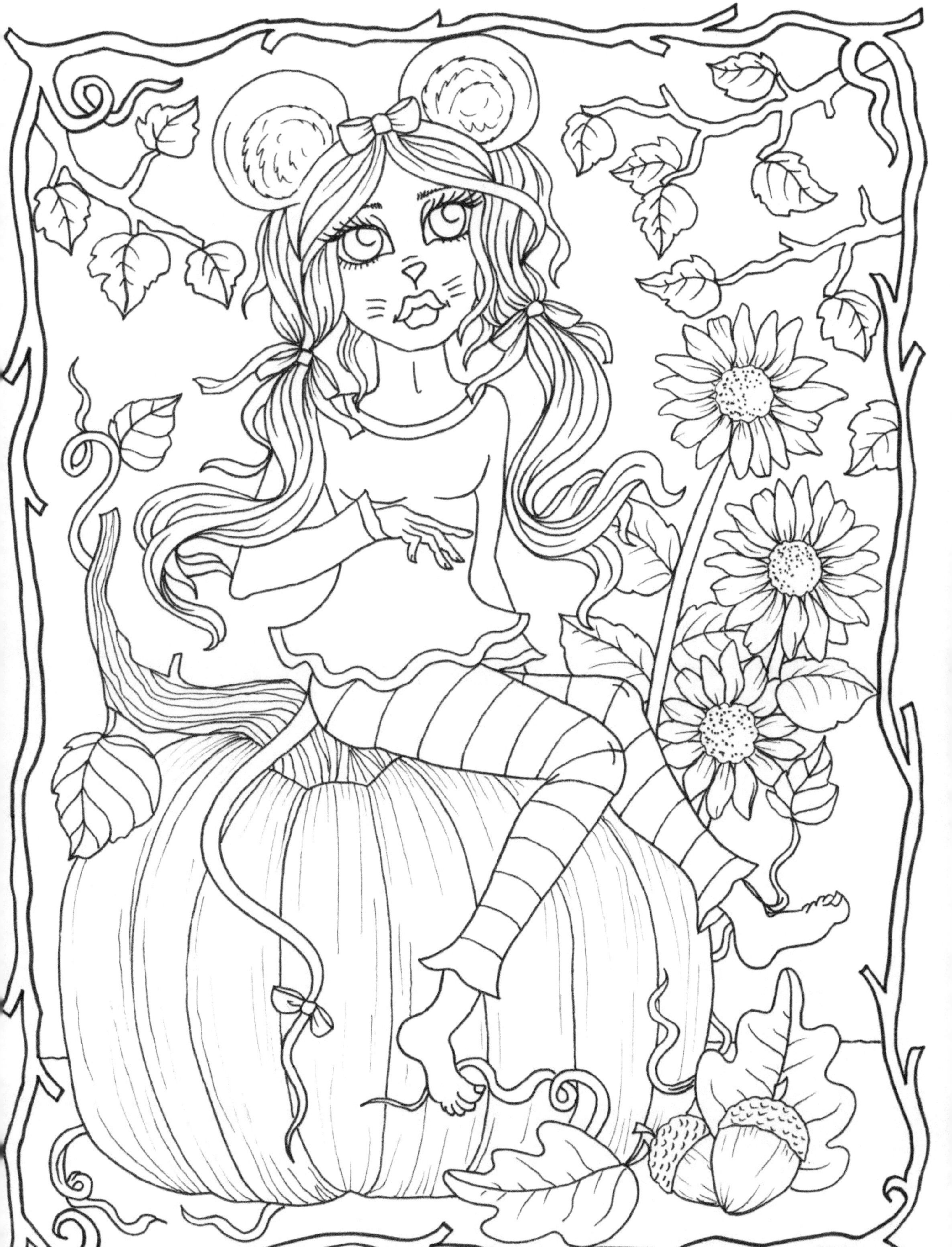

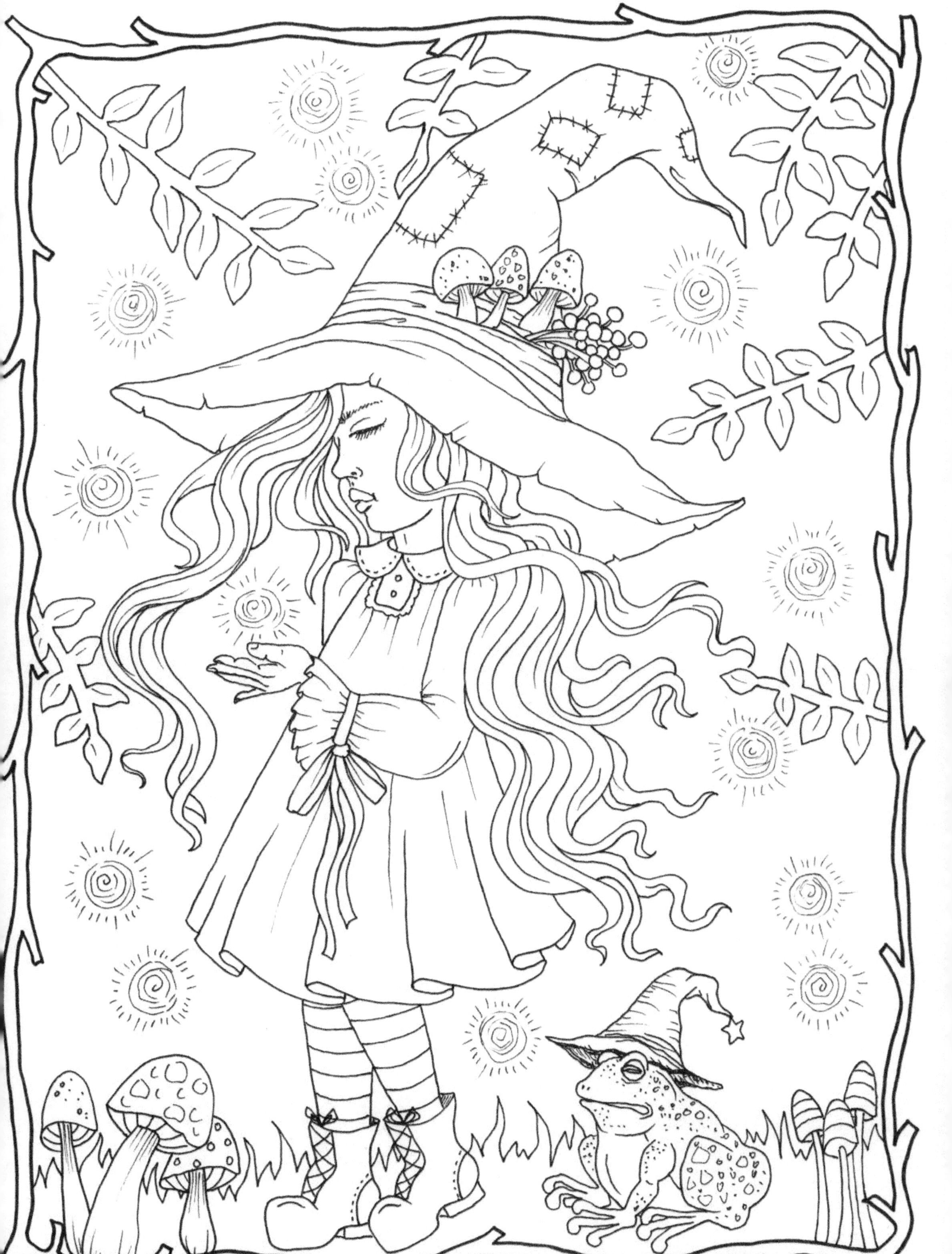

NOVEMBER

NOTES

My Color Palette

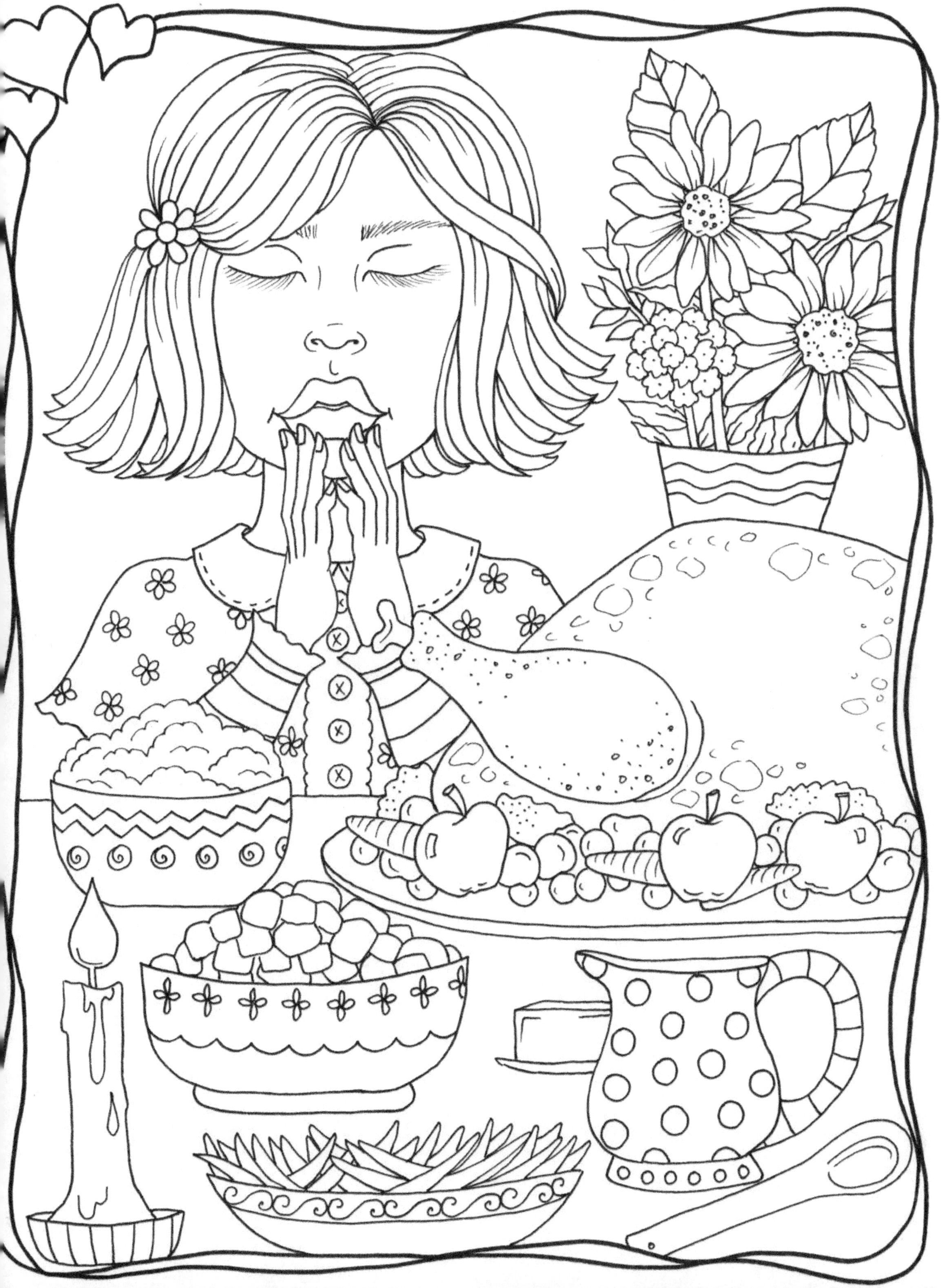

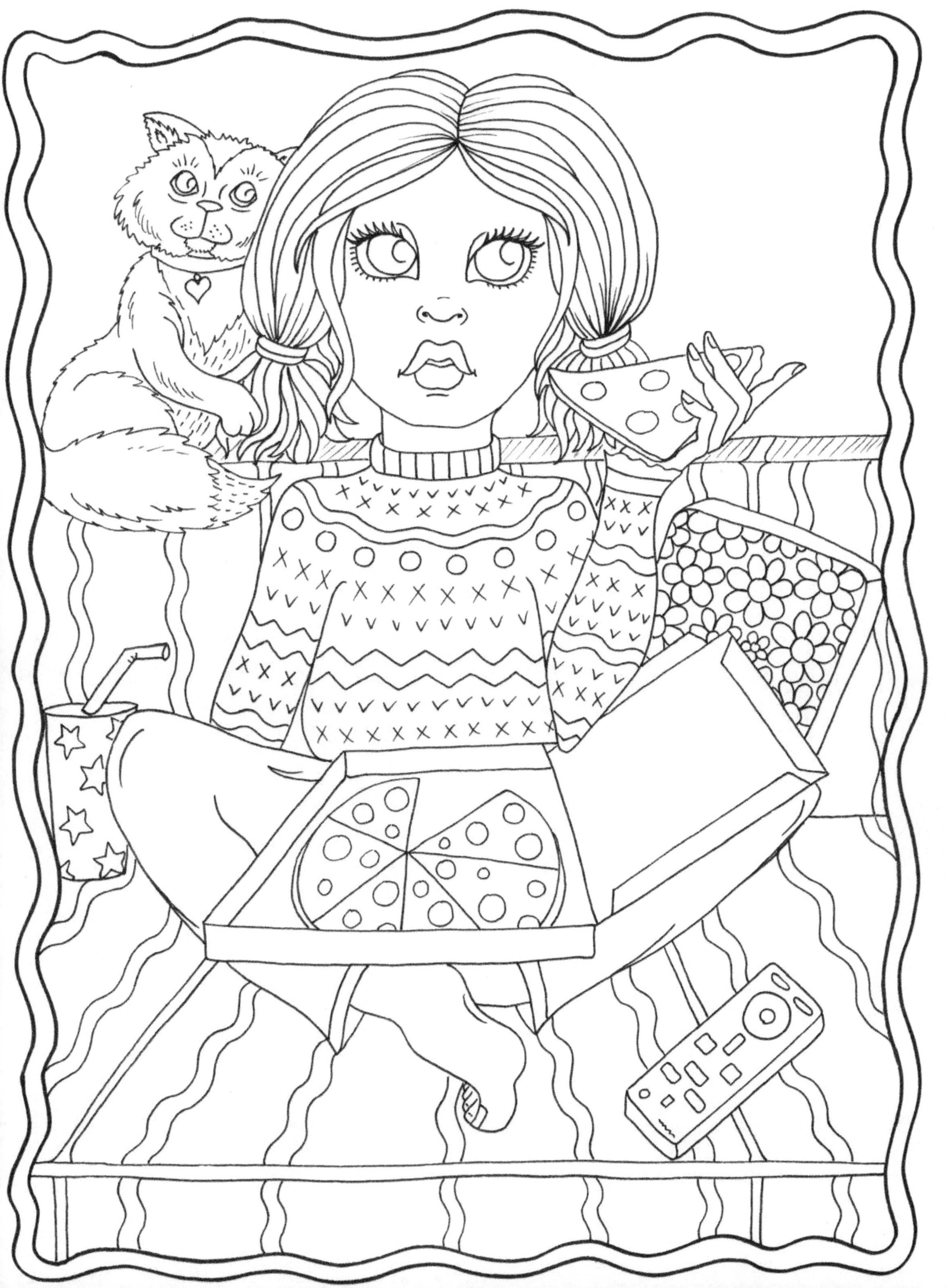

DECEMBER

NOTES

My Color Palette

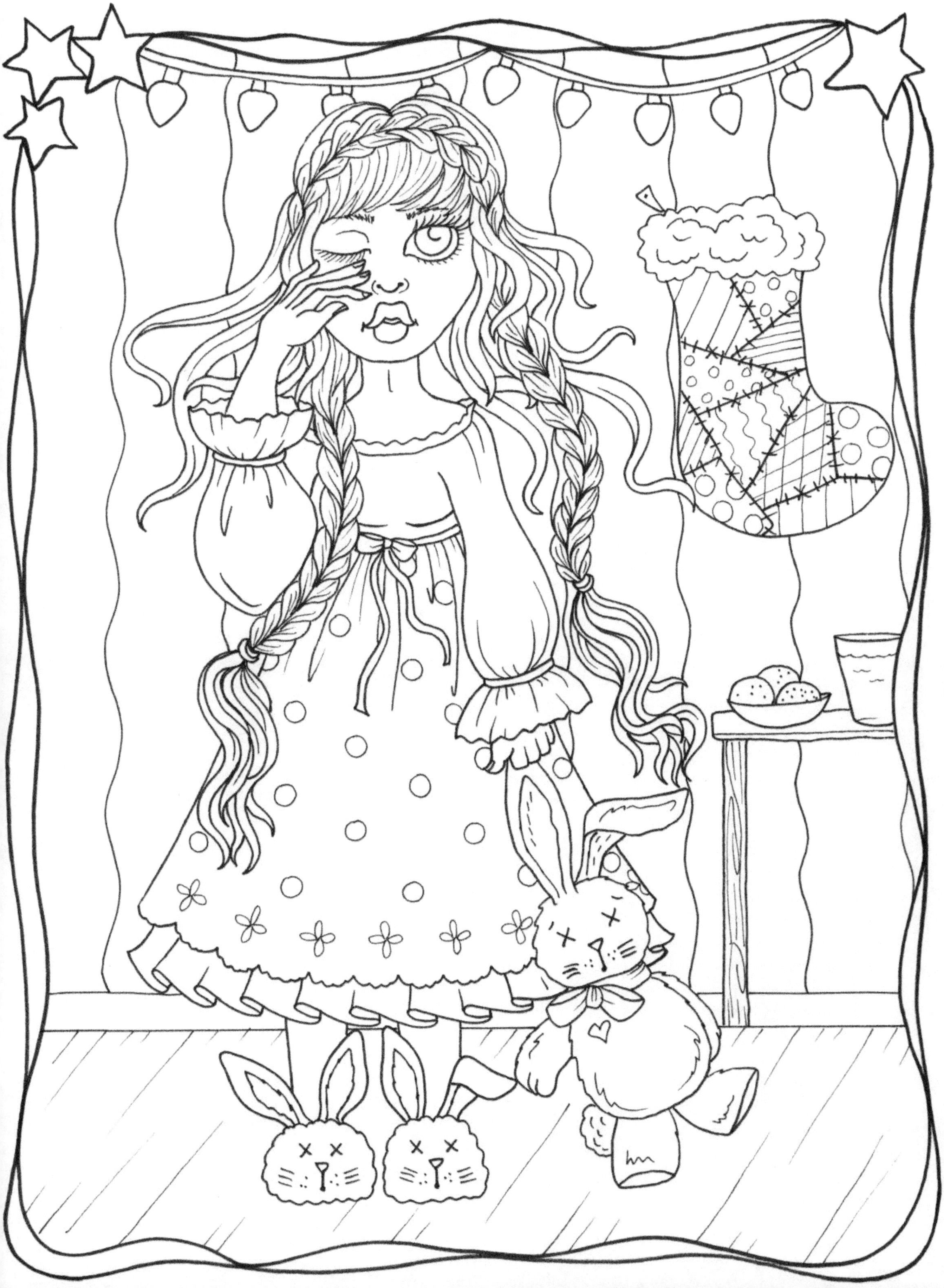

HANUKKAH

Thank you for purchasing this coloring book, one of many from Deborah Muller/Chubby Mermaid. Please don't forget to sign into your Amazon account and leave a review for Deborah Muller Coloring Books. Reviews on Amazon are essential to an artists business and the only way to grow our sales. Thank You!

★ ★ ★ ★ ★ ★ ★ ★ ★ ★ ★ ★

Follow me on Facebook
Chubby Mermaid Art by Deborah Muller

Join my Coloring Group on Facebook
Deborah Muller's Coloring Group

Instagram
Chubby Mermaid Art

Etsy
Chubby Mermaid

Pinterest
Deborah Muller Chubby Mermaid Art

Email
Chubbymermaid@hotmail.com

Website
ChubbyMermaidArt.com

Made in the USA
Las Vegas, NV
23 April 2025